SAVING WINSLOW

SHARON CREECH

SAVING WINSLOW

JOANNA COTLER BOOKS

An Imprint of HarperCollinsPublishers

Library of Congress Control Number: 2017962817
ISBN 978-0-06-257071-0

Typography by Laura Eckes
20 21 22 23   PC/BRR   10 9 8 7 6 5
❖
First paperback edition, 2019

For
Pearl and Nico
and
all you animal lovers

CONTENTS

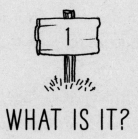

WHAT IS IT?

In the laundry basket on the kitchen floor was a lump.

"Another dead thing?" Louie asked.

"Not yet," his father said.

It was the midst of winter, when night, like an unwelcome guest, came too early and stayed too long, and when each day seemed smaller than the one before.

Louie's mother stared down at the basket that

her husband had brought into the house. "Another one of Uncle Pete's, I presume?"

Uncle Pete had a small farm on the outskirts of town. Anything to do with Uncle Pete usually involved Louie's father wasting time or money, or doing something dangerous like chopping down trees or racing tractors through mud fields, or disposing of dead animals. Louie's father had already brought home and buried two piglets that had not survived their birth.

Louie knelt beside the basket. A small gray head with black eyes and feathery eyelashes and sticking-up ears emerged. Attached to the head was a trembling thin body and four long spindly legs, all of it covered in splotchy gray fur scattered with brown freckles.

It was not a dog or a cat. It was a pitiful-looking thing and it was gazing at Louie. He felt a sudden rush, as if the roof had peeled off the house and the sun had dived into every corner of the kitchen.

"A goat?" he asked, kneeling beside the basket.

"No, a donkey," his father said. "A mini donkey, born last night."

"A mini donkey?" Louie's hand cupped the donkey's head, patting it gently. The donkey seemed too weak to move. "Something wrong with it?"

"The mother is sick, can't take care of it."

"Poor mama," Louie said. "Poor baby. What will happen to it?"

"Probably go downhill fast. Might last a day or two."

"No!"

"So," his mother said, "why do *you* have the donkey? Why did you bring it home if it might just die in a day or two?"

"I don't know," his father said. "I felt sorry for it. I thought maybe we could at least watch it until it—you know—until it dies." He whispered that last word.

The donkey made a small noise that sounded like *please*.

Louie lifted the donkey from the basket and held it close. It smelled of wet hay. It put its face against Louie's neck and made that noise again. *Please*.

"Okay," Louie said. "I accept the mission."

"What mission?"

"To save this pitiful motherless donkey."

SOMETHING DIFFERENT APPROACHING

Louie's house was old and cold and drafty and leaky, rising up out of its stone cellar with good intention but weakening as it reached the bowed roof topping the musty attic. The house was like many others on the narrow roads this side of town. Beyond the town stretched farmland and empty fields.

In summers past, the house had felt light and airy, with cooling breezes puffing the curtains in and out of the windows and always his older brother, Gus, there, so full of energy and purpose. "C'mon, Louie, let's paint the porch," and "C'mon, Louie, let's clean out that vegetable patch," and "C'mon, Louie, let's go to the creek," always with something new to do. But now Gus was in the army, gone already a year.

And now it was winter.

And each day short and dark and cold . . .

Until this snowy Saturday morning in January, with the wind plastering the windows with wet flakes, when Louie had awakened feeling *floaty*, suspended in the air, with something different approaching.

DON'T LET IT HEAR YOU

Louie had not had the best luck nurturing small creatures.

Those worms he brought into the house when he was three years old? Those cute wriggling things dried up and died two days later.

The lightning bugs so carefully caught and tipped into the glass jar with holes punched in the lid? Dead on the bottom of the jar three days later.

The lively goldfish won at the carnival? Belly-up

at the end of the week.

Blue parakeet also won at the carnival? Carefully fed and watered and talked to? Three months—then gasped its last breath at the bottom of its cage.

The kitten found at the side of the road? Ran away the second day.

The bird limping across the porch and gently brought indoors? Flew out an open window two days later.

Hamster? Snake? Turtle? Lizard? Louie tried, but all of them, each and every one, either shriveled and died or escaped.

More recently, he had been longing for a dog.

His parents thought it would be a better idea if he *borrowed* a dog from time to time. One that didn't *live* with them. One that didn't need walking in the rain and snow, and one that didn't pee on the carpet or chew on the furniture.

So Louie was more than a little surprised when

his father came home that Saturday morning with the pitiful donkey wrapped in a blue blanket.

"I don't want to watch it die," his mother said.

"No!" Louie said. "No dying. I told you, I accept the mission."

The pitiful creature tentatively touched its nose to Louie's. "Awww."

"Don't get attached," his mother warned. "You're going to be heartbroken when it—"

"Shh," Louie said. "Don't let it hear you." He asked his father if it was a boy or a girl.

"Boy," he said. "Poor thing."

His parents stepped out onto the front porch to "discuss the situation." Louie could see his mother waving her arms here and there, and his father nodding helplessly, shrugging his shoulders, as if he realized he had not thought this through. And then Louie saw him waving *his* arms and smiling and making a cute donkey face.

The pitiful donkey was trembling in Louie's arms, his wee head nuzzling Louie's neck, his long, spindly legs folded up awkwardly. By the time his parents came inside, Louie had a plan.

"He'll stay in the cellar. I can sleep there with him on the cot. Maybe we could have the heater on at night. We need to go to the feedstore and get some hay for him to sleep on and a bottle and some milk formula."

His mother's mouth opened and shut. No sounds came out.

"Mom? Will you watch him while Dad and I get supplies?" Louie handed the donkey to her, pushing him gently into her reluctant arms.

Louie's mother bent her head to the donkey, studying his sweet face. "Go on," she said. "But I'm warning you both. He may not last the night. And if he does, he may not last another day or two. You're going to be so, so sad."

"No!" Louie said. "I will save Winslow."

"'Winslow'?" Mom said.

"That's his name: Winslow. It just came to me, out of the air."

THINK POSITIVE!

Next door lived Louie's friend Mack, whose father owned the feedstore. Louie had been in the feedstore many times, helping Mack stock shelves, so he was familiar with the layout. He could direct customers to the cow halters, the livestock feed bins, the portable cages and tick repellent and vitamin supplements for animals of all types, and to books on every farm animal, from pigs to donkeys.

Mack was there when Louie and his father

arrived. They told him about the donkey and chose a suitable powdered milk formula.

"A small bag," Louie's father said, "because it probably won't live very—"

"Yes, it will," Louie said. "Don't say that."

Mack recommended a book, *All About Donkeys,* but Louie's father said they should get it from the library, "because, you know, what will we need it for if the donkey—erm—if it—"

"Don't say it! Think positive!"

That was pretty much how it was with the few items his father accepted: the smallest bottle, the smallest bag of formula, the tiniest vial of vitamins, the two-page free pamphlet titled *The Newborn Donkey* (instead of the two-hundred-page book, *All About Donkeys*), because he was convinced this would all be wasted on the pitiful donkey. His father did not want to buy a bale of hay for bedding, but Mack's dad offered to throw in a partial bale for free because it had fallen off someone's truck.

"We're going to feel pretty stupid," his father said, "if we get home and find a dead donkey."

"Quit saying that!"

"I just don't want you to get your hopes up."

MACK AND THE SISTERS

Mack was thirteen, three years older than Louie. People sometimes thought they were related because they were often together and both had dark, unruly hair and dark eyes and were tall and thin. Louie's own brother, Gus, shared Louie's dark features, but had their father's strong, stocky build. He had played football in high school and had been eager to join the army.

Louie missed him.

He sometimes missed Mack, too, because lately Mack had been hanging out with his friends from school when he wasn't helping at the feedstore. If Louie suggested sledding down the hill at the end of the road, Mack sometimes said, "Aw, I'm a teenager now, don't feel like sledding." But other times, if there was no one else around, he might join Louie and laugh his head off all the way down the hill.

It was while they were sledding that they had met the sisters, Claudine and Nora, who had recently moved to town and were the only other ones at the hill that day. It was late Sunday afternoon and the snow was packed and icy in spots. Later, Louie couldn't remember how it was that he and Mack learned their names and where they lived and that Claudine was Mack's age, and Nora was a year younger than Louie. It was all a blur, the way Mack and Claudine started talking and laughing while Nora and Louie kept on sledding down the hill, walking back up, and sledding down again.

On the way home, just the two of them—Louie and Mack—Mack put his hand over his heart and said, "I am in *love*!" He pretended to stagger and fall back in the snow.

DONKEY, DONKEY, IT'S OKAY

When Louie and his father returned from the feed-store, his mother was still cuddling the donkey, snuggling him in a blanket, stroking his head, and talking to him, "Donkey, donkey, it's okay."

Louie set up a place for Winslow in the cellar, with hay for bedding and blankets for extra warmth. Winslow was bleating pitifully, those little *pleas*: *plea-plea-please*. Winslow did not know what to do with the bottle of milk. He repeatedly bumped his nose against the nipple, and when he got it in his mouth, he spit it out. When it finally stayed in his mouth, he didn't know how to suck on it.

Louie stayed with Winslow, holding him, talking with him, petting him, coaxing him to drink. He dripped milk onto his finger and slipped his finger into Winslow's mouth. Winslow sucked on it eagerly. Louie repeated that until Winslow accepted the bottle.

Success! But it had taken two hours to coax an ounce of milk into Winslow, and then Winslow fell asleep. Louie, too, fell asleep, holding the blanket-wrapped pitiful Winslow.

When Louie was born, he was two months early and weighed only three pounds. He didn't like to see photos of himself from when he was such a scrawny birdlike thing, hooked up to tubes and housed in an incubator. He looked helpless.

Sometimes Louie thought that he could *remember* those early days. He knew that was unlikely, but often when he was falling asleep or waking up he felt as if he'd been gasping for breath and then suddenly his mouth opened wide and a rush of cool, clean air came in, and he expanded like a balloon, and he floated up and out of an incubator and into the world.

And such a world it was, full of blue sky and trees heavy with leaves every shade of green and birds swooping and diving and chirping and yellow tulips waving.

Louie was thinking about this when he fell asleep holding the pitiful donkey, and when he awoke a few hours later, he felt that rush of cool, clean air, but something was different; he did not feel floaty. There was the donkey, limp against his chest. Louie rubbed him with the blanket, begging Winslow to stay alive, please, please. Winslow's legs twitched. His eyes opened briefly and then closed again.

Louie urged the donkey to take more milk. "Please, Winslow, please?"

And he wondered, had his parents begged *him* to stay alive? Did they hover over him like he was hovering over Winslow? Did they urge him to keep breathing? Did they pat him and talk to him? And did that help him?

In two weeks, winter break would be over and Louie would have to return to school. He hadn't thought about what he would do with Winslow when that time came. How would he get frequent feedings?

His mother said, "Oh, don't worry about that. We don't even know if Winslow will be—"

"Don't say it."

AVOID THE BALL

Louie missed his brother, Gus, and wished he had not joined the army, even though it was what Gus had most wanted to do and everyone was so proud of him.

"You'll be serving our country," Louie's father had said.

Louie hoped he could serve his country, too, and he sometimes imagined himself standing on a hilltop, guarding the territory. Sometimes his arms were spread wide as if to shield everyone behind him. Was that serving?

Gus's favorite sports were basketball, baseball, soccer, and football, and although Gus had tried to interest Louie in these games, Louie gradually understood that he did not have Gus's natural talent. He was particularly wary of sports that involved balls. When he tried to throw, kick, dribble, or bat them, they rarely went where he intended. When someone else threw, kicked, dribbled, or batted a ball, Louie was unable to anticipate where it was aimed.

After one especially frustrating soccer practice, Louie's coach said, not unkindly, "Louie, you seemed to, um, *avoid* the ball."

"Right!" Louie said. "When it's coming at me, I don't know where to move. I can't get out of the way."

"You're not *supposed* to get out of the way."

"Yes, I am."

"Hmm. Maybe sports are not your thing, Louie."

Later that night, he asked Gus, "But what *is* my thing? If it's not sports, then what?"

"Don't worry, Louie, you have plenty of time to figure that out."

But Louie did worry. He feared he would never find something he was good at or something he was as passionate about as Gus was about sports.

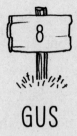

GUS

After his brother left for the army, Louie wondered how the absence of one person could take so much air out of the house. He kept bumping into empty pockets, spaces that Gus had previously inhabited: the couch with cushions squished; the kitchen counter always dotted with his sandwich makings—bread and mayonnaise and mustard and bologna and peanut butter; the bed across from his; the porch, cluttered with Gus's smelly shoes and sweatshirts.

All these places were now missing signs of Gus.

He and his parents hovered over each letter and postcard from Gus. They were hungry for his voice and his news, but he rarely phoned, didn't write often, and his news was not elaborate. Life was "okay" or "not too bad." Once he said it was "great!" but he did not explain why it was great. The food was "okay" or "not too bad," though one time he and his buddies had pizza. It was "great!"

"Not the biggest vocabulary," Louie's father observed.

At first, Gus had signed his letters simply "Gus," and then it was "Miss you, Gus," but lately, each letter closed with the same three words:

Remember me,
Gus

Of course they would remember him, Louie always thought when he saw that signature. What a crazy thing to say!

But it made him worry about Gus, and now, when Louie was holding Winslow, coaxing him to drink, wishing him stronger, he hoped that if Gus were sick or injured someone would watch over *him*.

WHAT'S THE POINT?

One morning, Louie's mother, standing at the top of the cellar stairs, announced visitors.

"Hey, Louie, we've come to see the sickly donkey!" It was Mack, clomping down the stairs, followed by Claudine and Nora.

Claudine rushed to Winslow. "Awww."

Nora stood a few steps back, staring at Winslow.

"May I touch it?" Claudine asked. "I could die from its cuteness."

Everything about Claudine was soft and elegant: her voice, her hair, her clothes. Even the way she stood was soft and loose.

Nora, however, did not appear soft. She looked as if she had crawled out of a shed, in dirty jeans and an oversized black coat and rather large black rubber boots. Her hands and feet seemed too big for the rest of her.

Nora did not say "Awww" when she saw Winslow. She said, "Ick." She looked around the basement, at the stone walls and concrete floor, at the buckets and hoses and rakes stacked in one corner, at the narrow cot, at Winslow's pile of hay, and then at Winslow. "Whatcha got that thing in here for? You sure it's a donkey? Doesn't look like a donkey. Looks like a possum-goat."

"A possum-goat? What's that?" Louie asked.

"A thing that looks like a possum married a goat and had a baby that came out like *that*."

"Don't mind Nora," Claudine said in her soft,

soft voice. "That's just the way she talks."

"Don't mind *Claudine*," Nora added. "That's just the way *she* talks."

Mack lifted Winslow from Louie's arms and studied him. "Gaining a little weight since I first saw him, isn't he? Still pretty spindly. Eyes are better though. Brighter. Maybe he's going to make it."

"Of course he's going to make it," Louie said, even though he was not sure from one day to the next. He felt it would be betraying Winslow, though, if he did not believe Winslow would make it.

"Little thing like that?" Nora said. "Doesn't seem half alive to me."

"He's still new," Louie said. He didn't know why he said that. It sounded dumb to him the minute it came out of his mouth. "Some newborns struggle to get going."

"Oh, I know all about *that*," Nora said.

"You do?"

"Sure. Our brother—"

Claudine interrupted her. "Oh, shush, Nora, your jabbering is bothering this poor little donkey. He's quivering."

"I am *not* jabbering, and I am *not* bothering that poor possum-goat." Nora looked Louie in the eye. "Our brother was born two months early—"

"So was I!" Louie said. "I was a pitiful, scrawny, struggling thing."

Nora touched Louie's arm with one finger. "But *you* made it."

"Oh." It was surprising, Louie thought, how much one simple sentence could affect your opinion of someone.

"Do you want to hold Winslow?" he asked Nora.

"Nope. What's the point?"

Claudine nudged her sister. "Cut it out, Nora. Don't be mean."

"I'm not being mean. I don't see the point of holding that thing if it's going to die anyway."

FREEZE THAT SCENE

One time in the middle of summer a year or two earlier, Louie was walking down the road on his way into town. He stopped near a batch of tall sunflowers blooming beside a white fence. It seemed like a painting to him: those bold golden sunflowers against that white fence and overhead a pure blue sky with white, white clouds drifting along.

Louie wished he could freeze that scene. Then, as he stood there perfectly still, a bird floated down and landed on one stalk. The bird was a deeper blue than the sky. *What shade was that?* Instantly the name *indigo bunting* came to his mind. He must have seen a bird by that name in a book, but he couldn't think when or where that might have been.

And now the scene appeared even more perfect to him: an *indigo bunting* atop a golden sunflower beside a white fence beneath a blue sky with drifting white clouds.

He felt supremely happy standing there.

On he went into town, to buy bread and milk. Before he reached the store, he passed the small park, and on one bench near the walkway lay a disheveled, thin man in a tattered army jacket. He appeared to be asleep. One arm was across his chest and the other hung low to the ground. The man was unshaven, his hair long and straggly, his clothes filthy.

Would I want to freeze this scene, Louie

wondered, *this scene of the unkempt thin man in a tattered army jacket on the brown wooden bench on the green grass near the gray walkway?* As Louie moved on, he thought he didn't have a choice. The scene, for whatever reason, was already frozen in his mind.

On his way back home, Louie slid a small brown bag next to the bench. In the bag were two rolls and a candy bar.

It was odd, Louie thought now—as he held Winslow trembling in his arms, the smell of milk formula on his face—it was odd that what floated into his mind were both scenes: the *indigo bunting atop a golden sunflower beneath a blue sky* and the *thin man on a park bench.*

Winslow's ears brushed against Louie's cheek. *This scene,* Louie thought, *will stay in my mind: little gray donkey in my arms, trying to stay alive.*

WHAT'S A WINSLOW?

One morning, when the snow lay deep and white on the ground and the sun shone overhead, Louie wrapped Winslow in a blanket and took him outside, settling on the front porch. Winslow became alert, turning his small head this way and that, eyes blinking against the bright light. He put his narrow face up to Louie's and nibbled at his scarf.

Beh-heh, beh-heh, he murmured. *Beh, beh, beh.*

It made Louie laugh. It was the first time the

donkey had managed that sound. Up until then, his whimpers had always sounded like *plea, please*.

"Do you think you're a lamb, Winslow? Are you going to *baa* like one? You're supposed to say *hee-haw*."

Winslow chomped on Louie's scarf, pulling strands loose.

Louie was rubbing his face against Winslow's when someone said, "Hey." Nora was standing on the sidewalk in her large black coat and her clunky black boots. On her head was a bright yellow knitted hat pulled low over her ears. Nora had big black eyes and black hair that poked out beneath the hat at peculiar angles. She looked rather like a bumblebee, Louie thought.

"What're you doing with that thing?" Nora asked.

"What *thing*? You mean Winslow?"

"What's a Winslow?"

"That's his name: Winslow. He's a donkey and

his name is Winslow."

"The one that's gonna die?"

"He's *not* going to die."

"Don't be so sure." Nora took a couple of steps toward the porch, tentative steps, as if she expected something to jump out at her or scold her and send her away.

"Want to hold him?"

"Naw. Why would I want to do that?"

"'Cause he's really soft."

"Naw."

Beh-beh-beh.

"Oh!" Nora said. "It makes a noise!" She had smiled automatically but then caught herself and removed her smile.

Winslow raised his nose in the air, smelling the air around this visitor. Within the blanket, his legs pedaled.

"He's squiggling," Nora observed.

"I think he wants to get down on the ground,

but I don't know—it might be too cold for him."

Nora was now standing at the bottom of the porch steps. "You could try it. Maybe. You could set him down on this shoveled part and see what happens. Maybe. If you want. Or not."

Louie unwrapped the blanket and set spindly Winslow down. He wobbled, his long legs bending this way and that until he managed to stand upright. Winslow turned toward Nora and took two steps, stopped, tottered, and then stumbled the rest of the way. He leaned against her, nudging her boots until Nora leaned down and patted Winslow's head.

"I think he likes you," Louie said.

"Naw. Naw." She patted Winslow again. "You think? Naw. Donkeys just do that, I bet, stumble at anybody."

"Maybe."

"Well, I gotta go. Here, you better wrap him up again. You know what I bet?"

"What?"

"I bet you could let him run around inside the house—I mean like upstairs instead of the basement—if you put diapers on him."

Louie winced. "Diapers?"

"Yeah, I heard about some lady who did that with a lamb, you know, so it doesn't stink up your house and make a mess."

"Diapers?"

"Yeah, diapers. I gotta go."

Louie watched her leave, in her big black coat and boots and that bright yellow hat.

HERE COMES TROUBLE

The rumble of Uncle Pete's old blue truck announced his arrival. Uncle Pete was a large man, tall and stout, with mammoth hands and feet. His normal greeting was a booming "Hey, there!" followed by a pat on the shoulder, but the pat was so forceful it usually knocked Louie off-balance.

"Hey, there, Louie! Whoa, careful there, don't fall over. You need some meat on those bones, boy."

Uncle Pete was a childhood friend of Louie's

father, not really an uncle, but that's how Louie's parents had always referred to him.

"Here comes trouble," Louie's mother said. That's what she usually said when she saw Uncle Pete.

"Ha ha! That's me, Trouble is my middle name." His cheeks were red from the cold. "Wicked out there today. How's that poor donkey doing? Did it croak on ya?"

"It was doing good until this morning," Louie said. "Come and see."

Louie had fed Winslow late the night before and the two of them had settled down to sleep, Winslow in his small pen and Louie on the nearby cot. Usually the donkey woke him up around four a.m. for another feeding, but Louie had slept soundly through the night without hearing Winslow.

When Louie did wake, it was almost seven o'clock, and he felt relieved. Now maybe Winslow would continue to sleep through the night. For the past week, Louie had been groggy all day long, never feeling fully awake, always feeling as if he could fall asleep sitting up.

When he opened the pen, Winslow did not scramble to his feet or turn his head toward Louie as he usually did. He made no sound, no *please*s, no *beh*s. He was lying on his side, his breathing shallow. When Louie lifted him, Winslow slumped in his arms, still not waking.

Louie rubbed his sides with the blanket and dipped a cool cloth against his face. "Aw, Winslow, c'mon. What's the matter? What's wrong?" Louie tried to recall if he had done anything wrong, if he had mixed the formula incorrectly, or if the bottle had not been clean. But he could not think of anything he had done differently the night before.

He summoned his parents and ran next door to get Mack's father, who was not a vet, but he knew about animals.

Mack's father said, "Some kind of infection

probably. Need to have a vet check him. Get some antibiotics in him."

"Did I do something wrong?" Louie asked. He hugged Winslow to his chest, stroking his head.

"Newborns are fragile," Mack's father said. "They can catch any old thing drifting through the air. It's a wonder any of them make it."

Mack's father called a good friend of his, a retired veterinarian, who came over right away. After examining Winslow, the vet gave him two shots and left a prescription for additional medicines.

"It's okay, boy," the vet said to Louie. "He might make it, but if he doesn't you're doing as much as you can. These things happen. You can do everything right and yet—"

His unfinished sentence hung in the air.

Before leaving, the vet said, "You'll have to give him one of these shots each day for at least ten days."

"What? Who? Me?" Louie said.

"I'll show you how. My grandson can do it, and he's only nine."

"Give a shot? You want *me* to give a *shot*?"

"Watch." He showed Louie how to fill the syringe, check the level, tap it to release air bubbles, insert the needle, and release the medication. "Practice on an orange. You'll be fine."

"But—but—"

"You can do it."

By the time Uncle Pete arrived later that day, Winslow was a little more alert. He had taken a few ounces of milk and had opened his eyes, but he still had not stood and was still breathing shallowly.

Uncle Pete touched Winslow gently, his huge hand enveloping the donkey's body. "Yep," he said. "He's a sick one. Too bad. Kind of amazing you got him to live this long, though."

"But he's going to make it," Louie said.

"Well—his mother didn't make it. My LGD died yesterday. That birth must have been harder on her than I thought."

"But Winslow will make it," Louie insisted. "He will. He will."

Later that day, Louie remembered that Gus had once told him that LGD meant Little Gray Donkey.

"Winslow, you are my LGD, and you're going to make it. Right?"

WHAT'S THE MATTER
WITH HIM?

"Louie? You awake? That girl is out front," his mother said. Louie was lying on the couch with Winslow wrapped in a blanket on his chest.

"Which girl?"

"You know, the one you call the bumblebee girl."

"Oh. Nora. What's she doing?"

"Walking back and forth. I think maybe she wants to come in or something. You'd better see for yourself. I'd probably scare her off."

Louie carried Winslow to the door. Sure enough, there was Nora walking back and forth on the sidewalk in front of his house.

"Hey," he called to her. "Did you come to see Winslow?"

"I was just nearby," she said.

"Well, do you want to see him?"

"Not really. No. Maybe. You got him there in that blanket?"

"Come on in," Louie said. "I can't bring him out today, but you can come in if you want."

Nora glanced up the street and down the street and kicked the snowbank with her boot. She was wearing her usual outfit and Louie realized he did not have a very good idea what she really looked like because she was always swallowed up in that big coat, and her hat was squashed all the way down on her head. He didn't know if she was plump or skinny or if she had long hair or short.

48

She came slowly up the walk, as if making up her mind whether she was going to come in or not. Louie opened the door wider.

"C'mon," he said. "Can't leave the door open. Might get Winslow cold."

"Okay, then," Nora said, stepping inside. She stomped the snow off her boots and casually tried to peer over the edge of the blanket-wrapped bundle in Louie's arms. "What's the matter with him? Something's the matter, isn't it? I can tell. He's all saggy."

"He's been sick."

"I knew it."

"What?"

"I just knew it." Nora stomped one foot hard on the floor. "It makes me so mad! I don't want to see it. I knew it."

"Wait—"

"I gotta go. I gotta. I knew it."

And with that, Nora left, stomping her boots all the way down the walk and down the street.

SEE THAT LIGHT?

One time when Louie was young—maybe three or four—he woke in the middle of the night and saw that the sky outside his window was silvery white, so bright. Through the window streamed a rectangle of light, a wide beam across the room. It fell across the foot of his bed and onto the floor.

He thought he was in a different world, maybe one where the sun shone silver. Maybe it was day and not night.

Louie went to the window and saw that the silvery light spread across the whole sky. The trees cast long, dark shadows across the lawn.

He walked through the house, peering out other windows, and everywhere was the silver sky, and everywhere the dark shadows.

He woke Gus. "Something is happening. See that light?"

"It's only moonlight," Gus said. "There's a full moon tonight."

Gus led Louie to the other side of the house, and there, from a bathroom window, above the roof of the neighbor's house, a full moon was suspended in the sky.

"See?" Gus said. "Nothing to worry about. Nothing unusual."

When he returned to his bed, Louie thought, *Nothing unusual? That silver light is not unusual? Then why had he never seen it before? Why did the light wake him?*

SHOTS

The first time Louie gave Winslow a shot, he almost fainted. He kept telling himself, *I can do this, I can do this*, but he didn't truly believe it. He was afraid of getting it wrong and hurting Winslow. He could hardly bear it that Winslow was sick, but it would be even worse if he hurt him more.

His father held Winslow while Louie prepared the syringe. For a moment, Louie felt dizzy and queasy. He thought he might vomit as he injected the needle and released the medication. Winslow briefly twitched, but he made no sound.

"Did I do it?" Louie asked his father. "I did it, didn't I?" He gently massaged the area around the injection site and held Winslow close.

"You sound surprised," his father said.

"Well, I am. Surprised and relieved."

"Me, too," his father said. "Surprised and relieved."

"I thought I was going to throw up."

"Me, too. I thought we *both* were going to throw up."

The next time he had to give Winslow a shot, he tried to convince his father to do it, but his father said, "No, you're taking care of him. You can do it."

That time, when Louie inserted the needle into the pinch of skin as he'd been directed, the needle went through to the other side and the medicine shot into the air.

Louie wanted to throw the syringe on the ground and shout, "I can't do this! I can't, I can't, I can't!" but one look at pitiful Winslow made him try again.

This time the needle went into the muscle instead of into the layer just beneath the skin. Winslow yelped and Louie cried.

"I'm sorry, Winslow! I don't want to hurt you. I can't do this. I can't make you better."

Louie felt helpless.

He imagined himself in the incubator when he was born. Was he pinched and poked and prodded? Was it hard to get a needle or a tube into him? Did he cry? Did the doctors and nurses feel helpless? Did his parents cry?

There was a lump in the muscle where Louie had misdirected the shot, and Winslow flinched when Louie rubbed it.

The next shots were easier, but Winslow was slow to respond to the medicine.

"Why doesn't he get better right away?"

"It takes time for the medicine to work," Louie's father said.

"But what if it doesn't work?"

Louie wanted Winslow to get better immediately. He hated not knowing if he was helping or hurting Winslow. He hated not knowing if Winslow would survive.

Sometimes Louie felt that saving Winslow would also save and protect Gus, like the two were connected somehow.

One day, Mack and Claudine appeared at the door, calling out for Louie. They were surprised, when Louie answered the door, to see Winslow making his wobbly way down the hall behind him.

"Unsteady, but at least he's walking," Mack said.

"Awww," Claudine said. "Diapers!"

It was true: a donkey with diapers. Inside the house. Upstairs, not in the basement.

"I know it's weird," Louie said. "But whenever I come upstairs from the basement, he looks so sad and bumps his head against the steps, over and over."

Claudine put her hand on Louie's arm. "But you have to, you know—you have to *change* the diapers?"

"Erm. Yes. Not my favorite job. I also have to give him shots."

"Shots? You know how to do that?"

"Still learning."

Claudine stroked Winslow's head. "Will he make it?"

"He'll make it," Louie said. "He will."

Claudine tilted her head sympathetically. "I guess I wouldn't get too attached, though. If it were me, I mean. I would be so, so upset if, you know, if—"

Louie interrupted her. "Hey, where's Nora?"

Claudine patted Louie's arm. "Oh, she didn't

want to—you know—"

"What? 'You know—' what?"

"We should leave, Mack, right? Don't you have to do that—that—thing—at the—?"

Mack blinked a few times and said, "Oh, sure. Better go. See ya, Louie. Talk to you later—"

Louie watched them head toward Mack's house next door. Claudine was in front and Mack behind her as they followed the narrow shoveled path. The way Mack followed Claudine reminded Louie of Winslow trailing behind him all day long.

ARE ALL DONKEYS SAD?

Louie did not like to leave Winslow when school resumed after the winter break. He fed Winslow before he left the first day and tucked two stuffed animals in the pen with him, along with one of his own shirts that had his smell on it. His father and mother would take turns coming home from work for the noon feeding and then Louie would be home after school for the next ones.

All day long Louie thought about the donkey.

Was he okay? Was he warm enough? Was he lonely? Louie could hardly concentrate on anything else. He doodled donkeys in the margins of his papers.

In the school library, he searched for books about donkeys, but found none. There were books about dogs and horses and sheep and cows, but no donkeys. The librarian handed him *Winnie-the-Pooh*, opening it to a drawing of a donkey.

"There you go," she said brightly. "Eeyore! A very famous donkey."

Louie was embarrassed. He was way too old for this book, he thought, and he already knew about Eeyore, the sad friend of Winnie-the-Pooh.

Are all donkeys sad? Louie wondered.

Louie was relieved, after that first day back at school, when he returned home and found Winslow standing in his pen, nose pressed against the wire, wagging his fluffy tail like a dog.

"Winslow! You're happy to see me, aren't you?"

Winslow wiggled and waggled and nudged Louie's face and neck.

"You're not sad, are you?"

Winslow burst out of the pen and flopped into Louie's lap, his legs collapsing in a tangled heap, his big, sticking-up ears tickling Louie's face.

YOU DON'T HAVE
TO DO THAT

Louie rarely saw Nora at school, but when he did she was often alone, either trailing down the hallway after her classmates or seated by herself at lunch. He hadn't recognized her at first, without her big coat and hat and boots. One day at lunch he sat down across from her with his tray.

"You don't have to do that," she said, studying her sandwich.

"Do what?"

"Sit there."

"I know that—I know I don't *have* to. Maybe I want to."

"Yeah, right."

They ate in silence, until Nora asked, "How's that thing—that sickly creature? Did it die yet?"

"It's a donkey. His name is Winslow. He did not die."

She looked up from her sandwich and said, "*Yet.*"

"He's really doing good," Louie said. "You should come by and see him again sometime."

"I'll think about it."

The following Saturday was sunny and warmer than it had been in weeks. Most of the snow had melted. Winslow was following Louie as he circled the yard.

"Maybe you should get a leash for it," someone said.

Louie turned to see Nora on the sidewalk.

"If you get a collar and a leash," she said, "you could walk it like a dog."

"Not a bad idea," Louie said.

"I've got a collar and a leash at home."

"You do? You have a dog?"

"*Had. Had* a dog."

"I'm sorry," Louie said. "That stinks."

"What stinks?"

"You know, that you *had* a dog—but now you don't—so it must have—did it, erm, I guess it died, right?"

"Well, it could have run away," Nora said.

"Oh, it ran away?"

"No, it died."

Sometimes when Louie talked with Nora, he felt as if she were speaking a foreign language.

"Do you want to pet Winslow?"

"Why'd you call him Winslow?"

"I don't know—it just came to me when I first saw him."

Nora removed a glove and tentatively patted Winslow's neck. He waggled his head and twitched his ears.

"That means he's happy," Louie said.

"Maybe," Nora agreed, "or maybe he waggles his head at any old thing."

REMEMBER ME

Louie found one of Gus's postcards on his book-shelf. It had been propped up there but had slipped between books. He liked rereading Gus's words. Even though Gus rarely said anything important, seeing his handwriting and reading his words made Louie feel as if Gus could walk into the room at any time.

* * *

Hi everybody,

I'm sorry I haven't written for
the last couple weeks. We have been
in some hard training and I fall into
my bunk every night, too tired to read
or write or . . . think.

I don't have any news so I'll sign
off for now.

Remember me,
Gus

THE GIRL WITH
THE YELLOW HAT

One Saturday morning, after a fresh snowfall the night before, Louie's mother said, "Nora is out there again. Why doesn't she come to the door? Are you supposed to *sense* that she's outside?"

Nora was walking back and forth in front of the house, swinging something—a rope?—in her hand.

"Nora? You want to come in?"

"I was just walking by. I brought the leash."

"The leash?"

"For the donkey. If you want to walk it. Or not.
I have a collar thing, too. You know what else?"

"What?"

"You could take the donkey over to the sledding hill."

That is how Louie and Nora ended up taking
Winslow for a walk down the street, in a dog collar
and leash, and towing a sled to the sledding hill.

"Try it with Winslow," Nora said. "Go on. He
might like it."

Louie bundled Winslow in his arms, climbed
on the sled, and, with a push from Nora, off they
went, careening down the hill.

Winslow's ears flapped crazily in the wind,
slapping against Louie's face. The sled swerved left
and then right and then straight down the last, fast
slope.

"Wow!" Louie shouted.

Nora was standing at the top of the hill,

clapping her gloved hands together, a bumblebee beacon in her yellow hat and black puffy coat and black boots.

"Your turn," Louie urged.

"Naw. Naw."

"You *have* to. And Winslow wants another turn, so here—" Louie shoved Winslow into Nora's arms and held the sled ready.

"Well, if I *have* to—"

And all the way down the hill came the strangest sounds: *urrrrawwp* and *urrrrawwp,* and only half of those were coming from Winslow. The rest were from Nora.

LOVESICK

Louie ran into Mack on his way home from school one day. Mack was not his usual peppy self. His head hung low, his arms limp at his sides.

"Hey, Mack, what's the matter? You look— terrible."

"Thanks for the compliment."

"Are you sick?"

"Yeah, I'm sick." Mack placed both hands on his chest. "Lovesick! I'm a goner."

"Claudine?"

"Yes, Claudine, Claudine, who else but Claudine? She hasn't spoken to me in two days. Two days, Louie! That's an eternity."

"You make her mad?"

"She said I was starting to suffocate her! Too much attention! Can you imagine that? How can you give a person *too much attention*? I thought that's what girls wanted: attention."

Louie had never thought about what girls wanted or even what boys wanted or if there was a difference or if it depended on each person. The only time Louie could recall feeling *too much attention* was in second grade. A new girl who did not speak much English had attached herself to Louie on the first day.

"Say me Cookie," she said, clamping on to Louie's arm. "Is bester name."

The teacher seemed pleased that Cookie had found a friend so quickly. She asked Louie to sit next to Cookie and to explain things to her and to show her around the school.

"Me?" he said. "Are you talking to me?"

"Of course, Louie, I am talking to you. Thank you for welcoming Cookie."

From that moment on, Cookie did not leave Louie's side except when she or he went to the bathroom. She followed him from the moment she saw him in the school courtyard in the morning until the bell rang in the afternoon. She probably would have followed him home except that she rode a bus to the other side of town and Louie walked home.

After three weeks of Cookie's attention, Louie had confessed to his mother, "I can't stand it! Cookie is always breathing in my face or asking me questions or following me around or hanging on my arm. I can't go back there!"

"Maybe you should mention to your teacher that you need a little break from Cookie."

"How can I do that, when Cookie is always

there, latched on to me?"

"You'll find a moment, I'm sure."

And he did find a moment a few days later, when Cookie went to the bathroom. Louie raced to his teacher and blurted out his dilemma, begging her to rescue him from Cookie.

"Hmm," his teacher said. "I suppose one day you might long for such attention, but I understand. I'll encourage Cookie to make other friends."

And Cookie did gradually make other friends and soon she hardly seemed to notice Louie at all, and although he felt relieved, he also felt puzzled. Didn't she like him at all anymore?

Now, walking home with Mack, who was lovesick for Claudine, Louie said, "Aw, leave her alone for a few days, see what happens. Maybe she'll miss you."

"When did you get so wise?" Mack asked, giving Louie a shove.

"Maybe it's from hanging around Winslow.

Come on, come see him, he'll make you laugh."

Winslow stumbled into their arms and flapped his floppy lips, and when Mack left, he was laughing.

"That donkey!" Mack said. "That donkey cracks me *up*!"

A PAINTING

Above Louie's bed hung a painting—or rather a copy of a painting—of a boy tugging on a rope tied to a calf who was resisting being led. It looked like a gentle tug-of-war between the boy and the calf, each equally determined. Behind them were golden haystacks and open fields with chickens pecking here and there. Two other boys stood near, watching the boy and the calf.

Another copy of this painting had hung in the

hospital waiting room outside the infant intensive care unit where Louie's parents had spent many hours after he was born. Something about the struggle of the boy and of the calf had spoken to them and calmed them. The artist's name was Winslow Homer.

SOMETHING THE MATTER?

It was spring, the early days of spring, when the shock of bright green sprouting from the ground and from trees was new and cheery, and when daylight was filtered through a gauzy curtain. Louie was out in the yard with Winslow, who was galloping about clumsily, and it was one of those good days, when everything seemed right with the world.

Nora came by. She said she was "just out walking," which is what she always said. She appeared smaller and more vulnerable without her heavy black coat and boots and yellow hat, and as she came through the gate she seemed worried.

"Something the matter?" Louie asked.

"Naw. Not really."

Winslow eagerly bumped his head against her arm until Nora petted him. She smiled, in spite of herself.

"He's so used to you now," Louie said. "I think he was expecting you—he kept looking up and down the street."

"Aw. Makes me sad."

"Sad? Why sad? I thought you'd be happy about that."

"Well, what's going to happen to him? Mack said you can't keep him here much longer. He's getting too big and too loud—"

This wasn't a surprise to Louie. His parents had brought it up earlier in the week. Winslow *was* getting big and even the makeshift pen they'd added to the back of the garage did not have enough room for him, and his new, loud braying was becoming annoying, not only to the neighbors, but also to Louie's parents.

Nora leaned her head against Winslow's neck, her own black curls mixing in with Winslow's gray and black tufts. "I bet you have to get rid of him. He will never be this free and happy again. He will probably get sick and die of sadness."

Louie tugged at Winslow's head, pulling it away from Nora. "Why do you always expect the worst?" he said.

Nora pulled Winslow's head back toward her. "To be prepared. Why do *you* always stupidly expect the best?"

"*Stupidly?*" Louie yanked Winslow's head back again, wrapping his arm tightly around Winslow's neck. "I *don't* always *stupidly* expect the best. I *worry* about the worst, but I *hope* for the best."

Nora stood very still, her arms stiff at her sides.

"Well, you must be disappointed a lot."

"And you must be sad a lot."

"Am not. I'm realistic," she said. "And you're being mean."

"Am not." Louie leaned in close to Winslow's face. "Am I, Winslow? Am I being mean?"

Winslow's lips flapped and he sucked his teeth.

"See?" Nora said. "He thinks you *are* being mean! He agrees with me."

"No, he doesn't. He agrees with *me*."

Winslow butted each of them with his head and kicked his hind legs in the air.

A LETTER FROM GUS

A collection of Gus's postcards and letters was kept in a blue bowl in the living room. Every now and then, when Louie or his parents were especially missing Gus, they would select one to reread.

Louie chose one addressed to him to take up to his room.

* * *

Hey, Louie!

I miss you, Louie. Are you getting older? Don't get too old before I come home, okay?

I wish I could be there to see you and Mom and Dad. I miss home. What's this I hear about a donkey? Really? A donkey?

Today I ate a snake. Really. I had to kill it and cook it and eat it. Don't tell Mom.

Remember me,
Gus

Louie read the letter while lying on Gus's bed. When he finished, he pretended he was Gus lying there. He kicked off his shoes from the back, like Gus did. He tossed a pillow over at his own bed, like Gus used to do. He regarded Gus's trophies lined up on the bookcase and Gus's baseball hats, stained with sweat.

Louie opened the closet and smelled the smell of Gus on his clothes. He chose Gus's favorite football jersey—the black-and-red one with number 21 on it—and put it on. He stood in front of the mirror and said, "I am Gus!"

And then he lay down again on Gus's bed and felt the enormous absence of his brother.

DON'T GO

With the arrival of warmer days and nights, Winslow was now kept in a pen attached to the garage. Louie's father had fashioned an overhang that extended from the garage roof, and he had enclosed part of the pen to give Winslow shelter from wind and rain and sun. Another solution would have to be found soon because theirs was not a yard in which you could easily keep a donkey. Not only was the yard too small, but it was also too close to the neighbors.

Winslow was now practicing his braying, emitting croaky, loud honks and *eeee-awe*s throughout the day. Neighbors begged for mercy.

"The donkey is a cute fella, I'll give you that, but the noise he makes gives me a migraine—right here—behind my eyes."

"I think he's practicing a warning," Louie said, "when a stranger is around."

"You mean a stranger like the mailman? A deliveryman? A cat? A squirrel?"

"Sometimes he seems to be, uh, singing," one neighbor said.

"I've noticed that," Louie agreed.

"But it's awful singing. If that's singing, then he needs lessons."

Most annoyed was Mrs. Tooley, who lived next door, on the opposite side of Mack and his family. Mrs. Tooley had never been friendly, so it was not a surprise that she would complain. When Louie's mother had taken a pot of soup to her one day, Mrs. Tooley said, "No, thank you. I don't like neighbor stuff." There was never a sign of a Mr. Tooley, and only rarely were there other visitors.

In the fall, when Louie had offered to rake the leaves from her yard, she said, "Leaves, schmeaves, let them be."

In the winter, when Louie had finished shoveling their own sidewalk, he carried on shoveling Mrs. Tooley's. She opened the door and said, "I'm not paying you."

"That's okay."

"So stop it."

Now Mrs. Tooley complained about Winslow. She would fling open the kitchen window and shout, "That donkey wakes up the baby! Make it stop that noise!"

Mack's family did not complain, but Mack did mention that Winslow might prefer living with other animals. "What about your Uncle Pete's farm? Isn't that where the donkey came from in the first place?"

Louie could not bear the thought of Winslow leaving. Who would look after him as well as he did? What if Winslow got sick again? What if Winslow thought Louie was abandoning him?

At night, Louie looked over at Gus's empty bed and thought, *First Gus goes. Now Winslow?*

"Don't go, don't go, don't go," Louie whispered into his pillow.

WINSLOW WAS CURIOUS

Winslow was increasingly curious, testing his curiosity most often with his mouth. He ate through two power cords (fortunately unplugged) and nibbled plastic buckets, newspapers, and jackets. He licked an oil spill on the garage floor, munched on the doorframe, and chomped on an old tarp.

Winslow trotted from one thing to another, smelling and tasting. Every few minutes he returned to Louie and bumped him with his head, as if to say, "I am still here. Are you?"

"He's like a little lamb," Mack said. "He follows you everywhere. He probably thinks you're his mother."

"What?"

"Well, think about it. You're the only parent he has known. He doesn't even know what another donkey *is*. He doesn't even know that *he* is a donkey! He probably thinks he's a human, like you."

That night Louie dreamed that his own parents were donkeys. In his dream, he thought, *Then I must be a donkey, too!*

Winslow brayed, as if in response.

That sound: maybe it came from outside, and maybe it was in his dream. Louie could not be sure, for he was still in his dream.

WINSLOW! WINSLOW!

One morning, when Louie went out to the pen to feed Winslow before going to school, the pen was empty and the gate was open.

Did I forget to close it? Louie wondered. *I'm sure I closed it. I'm nearly certain I did. Did I?*

He dashed down the street and through back-yards calling for the donkey.

"Winslow! Winslow?"

His parents and Mack joined in the search. All along the street were calls of "Winslow! Winslow!" as they ducked in and out of driveways and poked in bushes.

No Winslow. No sign of him, no sound of him.

"I can't go to school," Louie told his parents.

"But we have to go to work—"

"Fine, but I have to stay and look for Winslow."

Mack said, "I'll stay, too. Louie and I can both look for Winslow, and if we find him—"

"*When* we find him—" Louie corrected.

"Okay, *when* we find him, then we'll go to school."

They returned to the pen to see if the donkey had left a trail of any kind, but other than the normal patches of scuffed earth where Winslow and Louie frequently walked, nothing seemed out of the ordinary.

"I hope he didn't wander into the road," Mack said.

"Don't think it. Maybe he's asleep in someone's garden."

And so they searched, up and down the street, up and down driveways, crossing backyards and front yards, their calls for Winslow bringing neighbors to their windows and doors.

"You lose your donkey?"

"Haven't seen any donkey around today."

"Who's Winslow?"

"Is Winslow your dog?"

Louie ran to the next block and the next and the next. He called for Winslow, louder and louder. Drivers asked if he was okay. Grandmothers came to their doors, peering out at this boy running through the neighborhood.

"Must've lost his dog."

"My dog used to get out all the time. I bet he's got a dog like that."

Louie felt increasingly desperate. He begged the air, "Please, please, Winslow, please, where are you?"

He tried to imagine where Winslow might go. He could be wandering around, lost and afraid. Louie had a sudden image of sledding down the hill with Winslow and being tickled by his ears.

The sledding hill? The snow would be long gone, the hill would be grassy, but maybe—maybe—Winslow had wandered that far.

And so Louie went in that direction. He was tired now. He could barely breathe, his insides so full of fear and worry and pain. He could not imagine losing Winslow. He did not want to let his thoughts go there.

He rounded the corner of the road and something caught his eye as he glanced up to the top of the hill. Something or someone was up there. The sun was behind it, and in the glare, all Louie could see was an odd, lumpy shape.

THE BEAR

Once, when Louie was four or five years old, he had an encounter with a bear. He was outside in the yard when he spotted the bear lurking beside the oak tree near the garage.

He wanted to scream but could not. No sound would come out of his mouth. He wanted to run but could not. His legs were numb; his arms were numb. He could not move.

It was windy. Branches were whipping back and forth, twigs snapping.

The bear moved closer to the tree.

Help! Louie tried to shout. *Help!* But he could only hear the scream in his head. *Maybe if I play dead, the bear will leave me alone. Maybe it will go away.*

Louie slowly lowered himself to the ground and curled into a ball. He held as still as he could. His arm itched, but he could not scratch it. He needed to cough but dared not.

The wind blew and the bear was still there, inching closer to the tree.

Louie lay still for a long time, so long that he fell asleep.

He was awakened by the bear pawing at his shoulder.

"No!" Louie shouted. "No, please, no!" And this time, the words came out of his mouth, and when he opened his eyes, he saw—not the bear—but his brother, Gus, nudging him.

"What's the matter with you?" Gus asked. "It's only me. You fall asleep out here?"

Louie looked around, searching for the bear.

"There!" he shouted. "Watch out, there's a bear—"

Gus followed Louie's stare and then slowly moved toward the bear.

"No, Gus, don't, don't—" As Gus continued across the yard, Louie grabbed his arm and tried to pull him back. "Gus, don't—"

But Gus kept going and when he reached the bear, he lifted it up and turned to face Louie.

"This? Is this your bear?"

He was holding a puffy brown jacket.

"It's probably Mack's," Gus said. "He's always leaving his stuff here."

Louie was so relieved that he thought he would faint, but he was also embarrassed. He'd been afraid of a *jacket*.

"Don't tell Mom or Dad," Louie said.

"I won't," Gus agreed. "One time I was afraid of a moth."

SHH, HE'S SLEEPING

The memory of the jacket-bear surfaced as Louie stared up the hill at the lumpy shape at the top. He was out of breath from his search for Winslow, and he was worried and frightened. He wished Mack were with him, but Mack had gone in another direction.

Louie slowly moved up the hill. He was approaching from the back side, not the sledding side, and the sun was in his eyes. He thought he heard humming.

Coming up the last stretch, he was able to see more clearly.

"Nora?"

She turned abruptly, putting her finger to her mouth. "Shh."

Nora was seated cross-legged on the grass, with Winslow beside her.

"Winslow! We've been searching—"

"Shh, he's sleeping. Very tired."

It was a maddening thing about Nora, and about most people who did not say much. Louie rarely knew what they were thinking or even *if* they were thinking. Sometimes he wanted to bore a hole in their heads and peer around inside. He felt as if he'd then be able to *see* what they were thinking. Maybe the words would be written across a large screen in their brains.

People who talked *too* much were also maddening to Louie. All those words pouring out of their mouths in gushing torrents: "blah blah blah blah

blah blah Did you know blah blah blah did you hear blah blah blah I felt blah blah blah I saw blah blah blah." When he encountered someone like that, he wanted to put his fingers to his ears to shut out the noise, and at those times, he wished the talkers were more like the quiet people. Maybe he would rather know less, not more.

On the hill, when Nora said, "Shh, he's sleeping. Very tired," Louie wanted to know so much more, but he was grateful that she offered at least those few words, and he was grateful—so relieved and so very grateful—to find Winslow.

QUESTIONS

Louie crouched beside Nora and gently stroked Winslow's head, relieved when Winslow's ears twitched. He was alive and he was safe.

"Thank you," Louie whispered.

"For what?"

"For finding him, for saving him. I was so worried."

"Shh. Why?"

"Why? Because he was missing and I thought

he was lost or hurt—he could've been run over—or fallen in the creek—or—"

"Shh."

All the while, Nora sat completely still, gazing down the hill. She was wearing a bright red sweater and her hair was piled on top of her head in a topknot, and she reminded Louie of a tomato.

"I have to take him home, Nora. We have to get to school." Winslow woke, blinked, turned from Nora to Louie, and flapped his lips.

"You woke him up."

"We can't sit here all day."

"I guess not. Here, then, you'll want this—" She handed Winslow's leash to Louie and raced off, running home.

It wasn't until Louie reached his own house, opened Winslow's pen, removed his leash, and went to hang it on its hook that he thought, *How did Nora get Winslow's leash?*

* * *

Louie was eager to see Nora at school and find out where and when she had found Winslow, but she was not in the cafeteria at lunchtime, and he did not see her among the crowds of students leaving after school.

When he arrived home, Mack was kneeling in Winslow's pen, talking to him, but as soon as Winslow sensed Louie approaching, he waggled his ears and let out a loud, gurgling *eeee-urp-awe*. Winslow buried his muzzle in Louie's stomach and munched on his sweater.

"I wonder when and how he got out," Mack said.

"I'm not sure when," Louie said, "but I think I left the gate unlatched. I must have." He was too embarrassed to admit he'd probably also left Winslow's leash attached.

"You ought to get a lock on this gate," Mack

said. "Anyone could come along and take him or let him out to run away."

"But he'd raise such a ruckus! He'd scare a stranger away."

It bothered Louie that Winslow had run away.

GUS FAN CLUB

Saturday morning was gloomy, with fog blanketing the house and yard. Louie rummaged in his closet until he found one of Gus's sweatshirts. It was thick and warm and still smelled of Gus.

When he entered the kitchen, his mother said, "Great minds think alike." She, too, was wearing one of Gus's sweatshirts. "Wait till you see your dad."

Before he could ask why, Louie's father emerged

from the basement. He was wearing Gus's varsity football jacket.

"See what I mean?" his mother said. "Look at us. We're a Gus fan club."

"Miss that boy," his father said. "Can't help worrying about him."

A faint knock at the front door startled them. Perhaps they were each thinking or hoping: *Gus! Could it be Gus?* Or worse, *Is it bad news about Gus?*

It was Nora, huddled in a bright yellow rain jacket with the hood pulled up over her hair. Her face was so small within.

"I was just walking," she said.

"Oh. Do you want to come in?"

"No. Well. I don't know."

"We're eating breakfast. Want some?"

"I ate." Nora looked left and right and up and down. "Maybe I'll go check on Winslow. That okay?"

"I'll come with you, show you where his food is. You can feed him if you want."

Winslow hopped onto a hay bale and then into the air and flung himself against Nora and Louie, hopping and wagging his tail and flicking his ears. He nibbled their sleeves.

"He's the funniest thing, isn't he?" Louie said.

Winslow's muzzle was pure white now and his coat pale gray. Down his spine was a darker stripe, and across his shoulders lay another dark stripe, making it seem as if he were wearing a cross. He wiggled and wobbled and darted here and there, between their legs, up onto the hay bale, leaping down again.

"I didn't see you at school yesterday," Louie said.

"Oh."

"I wanted to ask you—about finding Winslow—you had his leash—?"

"You didn't want him walking around these

roads without it, did you?"

"No, but—how did you get his leash in the first place?"

"You silly. It was right there on that hook in the pen."

HEY, THERE!

Uncle Pete's blue truck rumbled into the driveway, stopping near the pen.

Agitated by this stranger, Winslow brayed loudly and insistently, a combination of honks and gurgles and screeches.

"Hey, there!" Uncle Pete called.

Nora retreated behind Louie. "Who is *that*?"

"That's Uncle Pete. Wouldn't hurt a fly."

The imposing form of Uncle Pete, clad in a blue plaid shirt, overalls, and rubber boots covered in muck, did not reassure Nora.

"He's so *big*," she whispered.

"Hey, there," Uncle Pete repeated. "Who's your friend, Louie? How's the donkey? He sure has grown. I never thought he'd make it."

Eeee-urp-awe-honk!

Winslow backed up, shielding Louie and Nora from this big creature approaching.

"This is Nora. She found Winslow the other day when he got lost."

Uncle Pete put his hands on his hips. "Lost?"

"He didn't get lost," Nora said.

Eeee-urp-urp-awe-honk! Honk!

"What?" Louie said.

"He didn't get lost."

"But—"

"You kids. I don't know what you're talking

about," Uncle Pete said. "Your parents up yet, Louie?" He didn't wait for an answer, though. He tapped at the door and walked on in, calling out, "Hey, there! Got coffee?"

I'M CONFUSED

"Nora, what did you mean: You found Winslow's leash on the hook here in the pen? He wasn't wearing it when you found him?"

"No, of course not."

"So you heard Winslow was missing and came to get his leash?"

"No."

"I'm confused. And what did you mean, 'He didn't get lost'?"

Nora stroked Winslow, her fingers tracing the dark strip along his back.

"Sometimes I get up really early."

Louie wished Nora had a key on the back of her head so that he could wind it and make her talk faster.

"What does that have to do with anything?"

"When I get up early, sometimes I go for a walk."

"Great."

"Sometimes I come over and check on Winslow."

"You do? I've never seen you in the mornings."

"Early, really early. You're all still asleep probably."

"Nora—did *you* leave the gate unlatched yesterday?"

"Me? I don't know. Maybe."

It was still foggy in the yard, and for a moment, Louie thought that Nora resembled a phantom in her yellow raincoat with the hood over her head. Winslow was chewing on her sleeve.

"We have to be more careful," Louie said. "If he gets out again and wanders off—well, he could get hurt."

"He didn't wander off. We went for a walk."

"You *what*? You went for a *walk*? All that time I was so worried—you were out for a *walk*?"

"He looked so lonely in his pen. I thought a walk might cheer him up."

Louie hardly knew what to say, his head such a tangle of thoughts. He watched as Nora stroked Winslow's neck, the tips of her fingers sliding along so gently, her yellow sleeve against Winslow's gray coat. He couldn't be mad at her.

"Next time, Nora, leave me a note, okay?"

"Okay."

WE NEED TO TALK

When Uncle Pete emerged from Louie's house with Louie's father, Winslow seemed to accept that Uncle Pete was no longer a threat. He did not flinch when Uncle Pete patted his sides and peered into his eyes and ears.

"Yep, he's done okay. Never would have guessed it. He's probably ready."

"For what?" Louie asked.

Louie's father said, "Pete? Hold on a minute."

The two men walked over to Uncle Pete's truck, talking in low tones.

"What's he talking about?" Nora asked. "Winslow's ready for what?"

"A different kind of food, probably," Louie said. "Or a vet checkup."

At that moment a single shaft of sunlight pierced the fog and shone on Winslow's head.

"That's an angel at work," Nora said.

"What?"

"Everybody knows that."

Uncle Pete waved as he pulled out of the driveway.

From next door, Mack called out the window. "How's Winslow?"

"Good," Louie said. "You coming over?"

"Soon as Claudine gets here."

"My sister?" Nora said. "That Claudine?"

"That's the only Claudine I know."

"So, Mack," Louie said, "you two are speaking again?"

"Yep. Speaking and . . . *smooching*."

Nora said, "Ick!"

Winslow's reaction was harder to distinguish: *Eeee-urp, eeee-urp*.

On the other side of Louie's house Mrs. Tooley called out, "Shut that donkey *up*! Shut *up*!"

Louie's mother opened the back door. "Was that Mrs. Tooley yelling about Winslow?"

"Yep."

"Winslow annoying her again?"

"Yep."

The baby cried and Winslow brayed.

"Shut *up*!"

"Sorry, Mrs. Tooley," Louie called.

"I'm trying to get this baby to sleep!"

"Sorry." And then, under his breath, so that Mrs. Tooley could not hear him, he said, "Sometimes your crying baby wakes *me* up."

Louie's father joined them in the pen. "We need to talk," he said.

Nora said, "Uh-oh. Gotta go."

"You can stay," Louie's mother said. "It's okay."

"No, I don't like bad news."

"Who says it's bad news?" Louie asked.

I KNEW IT!

Winslow nudged Louie's hand, flapping his lips over it, slobbering, reaching for a carrot.

The way Louie's father was leaning against the side of the garage reminded Louie of Gus, the way he used to casually lean against things: walls, doors, fences. For a moment, Louie was cheered, thinking of Gus like that, but in the next instant, he missed his brother more than ever.

His parents looked worried.

"It's Winslow," his mother said. "We've had a long talk with Uncle Pete, and he agrees that Winslow needs to go."

"I knew it," Nora whispered to Louie. "I knew it was bad news."

Louie clutched Winslow to him. "Go? Away? Away from us?"

Louie's father rubbed his hand along Winslow's side. "We've talked about this before, Louie. We're not allowed to keep farm animals this close to town."

"But Uncle Pete has farm animals close to town."

"Not this close, and that area is zoned as farm land. Besides, Uncle Pete says donkeys need to be with other animals, not alone."

"He's not alone," Louie said. "He has me. Us."

Nora was holding on to Winslow's tail.

Louie's mother said, "He could go back to Uncle Pete's."

Both Louie and Nora pounced at once: "No!"

"But why not?"

Nora crossed her arms defiantly. "Tell them, Louie. Tell them why not."

Louie also crossed his arms. "Because he needs to be here. We need to protect him."

Mack came around the side of the house, hand in hand with Claudine.

"Hi, everybody, what's up?" Mack was swinging Claudine's hand back and forth, but he stopped when he saw the expressions on Louie's and Nora's faces. "What's the matter?"

Claudine placed her free hand against her lips. "Oh, no, is something wrong?"

"Yes, something is wrong!" Nora said. "You get attached to something and it always gets taken away! I knew it!"

DO YOU MISS US?

That night, Louie lay in Gus's bed, under the quilt that smelled like his brother. He wanted Gus to come home. He wanted to ask him things.

Are you afraid?

Are you hungry?

Are you cold?

Are you safe?

Do you miss us?

He wanted to tell Gus about Winslow, about

how he loved Winslow with all his heart. He wanted to tell him that Winslow understood things and that Winslow loved him back and that he was funny and goofy and occasionally loud, and Louie could not imagine life without Winslow.

Before Gus left for the army, Louie had not been able to imagine life without Gus, and then one day he was gone, leaving behind big empty spaces.

He wondered about what Nora had said: *You get attached to something and it always gets taken away!*

Something else was bothering him, too. Who did Winslow belong to? To Louie? Or to Uncle Pete?

HE'S NOT A DOG

The warmer weather brought out more walkers and joggers. If Winslow was in sight, they would stop and gaze at the donkey.

"Awww."

"It's a—a—donkey!"

"Cutest thing ever!"

Winslow responded by braying, a variety of loud, ridiculous, squawking, honking, shrieking sounds, and then Mrs. Tooley would call out,

"Shut *up*!" which would only make Winslow bray louder and more insistently.

One day, when Louie and his father were in the yard, an animal control officer arrived. The officer did not get out of his car. Instead, he lowered the window. He did not smile.

"Is it true you have a donkey on the premises? Is that it out back? Complaints have been made. This neighborhood is not zoned for farm animals."

The officer handed Louie's father a pamphlet outlining animal control regulations and a notice to remove the animal within seven days.

"Don't you even want to see Winslow?" Louie asked.

"Winslow?"

"The donkey. He's very friendly."

"I can see him from here."

Urr-onk-eeee-awe!

"I can *hear* him, too."

"He's not even as big as some dogs."

"But he's not a dog."

Louie's father said, "We're working on it."

The officer interrupted. "You need to remove the animal. Within seven days. Is that clear?"

He did not wait for an answer.

CAN HE *DO* THAT?

Louie erupted.

"What? Can he *do* that? Can he order us to get rid of Winslow?" Louie kicked at the driveway. "Who makes those rules? What is the *matter* with people? Couldn't he at least have looked at Winslow? Wouldn't he have realized that he is not a nuisance?"

As if in protest, the baby next door cried and Winslow answered: *Eeee-urrpa-awe.*

Mrs. Tooley opened her back door and called out, "Shut that donkey *up!*"

"Shut your *baby* up!"

Louie's father put a hand on Louie's shoulder. "Now, now—"

"I don't care! That screaming baby is a nuisance! Let's get rid of *it!*"

"Louie—"

"Stupid people. I *hate* people!"

"Louie—"

YOU HAVE A DONKEY?

Later that same day, another car pulled up in front of Louie's house. A woman in a khaki-colored uniform stepped out and then reached back inside for a clipboard. Louie froze. Was this about Gus?

She was as thin a person as Louie had ever seen, so thin you could see the bones of her hollowed face. You could see all the tendons in her neck as she stretched it forward, eyeing the house and Louie.

As she approached, Louie saw the badge on the pocket of her shirt. It read BOARD OF HEALTH. Beneath that was a small photo of the skeletal woman's face and a name: Dolores.

"You live here?" she asked. Her voice was crackly, as if it might disintegrate at any moment.

"Yes."

"Your parents home?"

"Yes."

Dolores checked her clipboard. "You have a donkey?"

"Yes."

Dolores tapped her clipboard with a pen and shook her head. "Can't have donkeys here."

"It's only a little one. No bigger than a dog."

From the backyard, sensing the stranger, Winslow let out a loud, croaking, honking *eeee-urrrr-awe, eeeee-urrrr-awe.*

"Oh, my. That sounds like a donkey, all right." Dolores started down the driveway toward

Winslow's pen as he continued to bray loudly and obnoxiously. "Can't have donkeys here," Dolores repeated. "Health hazard."

"But he's very healthy," Louie said. "Want to pet him?"

"Oh no. No, I do not. Health hazard." Her dark eyes were like tiny marbles set back in her eye sockets. "Ticks. Fleas. Fungi. Not to mention the bacteria in the feces."

It was difficult to hear over Winslow's loud protests.

"In the what?" Louie asked.

"The feces. The—the—poo. What is your procedure for dealing with the feces?"

Eeee-urrrpa-honka-awe! Winslow did not like this stranger. His mouth was right up against the fence, yelling at her.

From next door came the sound of the crying baby and the unmistakable voice of Mrs. Tooley: "Shut that thing *up*! Shut it up *now*!"

"Ah," Dolores said. "Complaints. I need to speak to your parents." She turned to the house and knocked on the back door.

Louie stayed outside as she spoke with his parents. Maybe she was only doing her job, he thought, but she didn't even seem to notice how cute Winslow was. She didn't know that he had struggled to survive, nor that he could be gentle and loving. She didn't notice that he had no ticks or fleas or fungi. She didn't care.

Louie hoped he would never have a job like hers, but if he ever did—if he was forced, say, to have a job like that—he would look the animal in the eye and he would kneel beside it and he would listen to the boy or the girl who was with the animal and he would never be cold or cruel or dismissive of the boy or girl or animal.

FOLLOW ME

Louie had never been to Nora's house. He knew what street she lived on, and that it was a short one, but he did not know which house was hers. Winslow, wearing a new halter, was at his side. Louie walked the length of her street, hoping that maybe she would be outside, and then turned and walked back down the other side, kicking at pebbles along the way.

"Stupid animal control officer! Stupid Board of

Health! Stupid regulations!"

He sensed that Winslow, at his side, sympathized.

"Stupid Mrs. Tooley! Stupid crying baby!"

"Hey—Louie!"

It was Nora, standing at the door of a small white house. She came down the walk, pulling on her jacket. "This way," she said, motioning to a path across an empty lot.

Nora paused to stroke Winslow's head and to let him slobber on her sleeve, and then she led the way through the lot and out onto a narrow dirt road. "It's a shortcut. Been here before?"

Louie was disoriented. "No, I don't think so. Where does it end up?"

"Follow me. You'll see."

There were not many homes along the dirt road. Most were small and old, some were trailers, and some abandoned.

"You've never been back here?" Nora asked.

"I don't think so—maybe a long time ago—I don't know. Where does it end up?"

"The dump."

"Oh. And then the main road is on the other side?"

"Yes."

They were not far along when Winslow stopped, alert, and brayed loudly. A dog chained to a tree in one of the yards barked ferociously in return. Winslow strained at the halter and continued to bray, unleashing a furious diatribe of *urp*s and *arp*s and *onka-onka*s.

A man came out of the house and smacked the dog with a newspaper. "Get that donkey out of here!" he yelled. "Go on, get a move on."

"Sorry," Louie said. "I never heard him like this."

The man shouted, "Donkeys and dogs don't get along!"

Louie and Nora managed to steer Winslow

away and down the road.

"Wow," Nora said. "That was ugly."

"Scared me a little," Louie admitted, "but I think Winslow was trying to protect us. Definitely not going by *that* place again!"

They decided to carry on to the dump and then return by the main road, but when they reached the road, Louie suggested they continue on to Uncle Pete's farm.

Nora put her hands to her chin. "I don't know. How far is it?"

"Not real close, but not too far."

"That's not real helpful, Louie."

"Come on, you'll like it."

"I might not. I don't guarantee I'll like it."

"But you might."

ARE THEY GOING
TO MAKE IT?

A long, wide dirt driveway led up to Uncle Pete's clapboard farmhouse. Louie steered Nora and Winslow around the side, toward the red barn in the back. Winslow's ears perked up, swiveling this way and that, taking in the sounds of the cows and the pigs and the sheep and the chickens, a lively barn song of *moo*s and *oink*s and *baa*s and cackles.

Winslow pranced and leaped, eager to investigate.

Nora's hands were pressed to her cheeks. "I don't know," she said. "I don't know if I can do this."

Uncle Pete waved to them from a tractor. "Hey, there! Go on, wander around. Check out the newborn lambs and calf! I'll be back soon," and he rumbled off on the tractor into an adjacent field.

In a smaller pen, separated from the rest of the sheep, was a ewe and her twin lambs, so tiny and scrawny, with short, sparse white hair revealing pink skin beneath. One lamb was standing and stumbling about, and the other was curled against its mother.

"That looks so much like Winslow when you got him," Nora said.

"Was Winslow really that little and that scraggly?"

"He was! Remember?"

Winslow pressed his nose against the wire pen and made the softest sound, a little like the *please* he had first uttered on the day that Louie's father had brought him home.

The ewe lifted her head, acknowledging Winslow, and answered him with a single *baa* before she bent her head to her newborn. The other newborn stumbled this way and that until it collapsed against its mother, joining its twin.

"Are they going to make it?" Nora asked. "I hope they're going to make it. But they seem so frail, don't they?"

"That's how they all are at first," Louie said, surprising himself with his own confidence. He had seen dozens of newborn lambs in the past, and he had often felt as Nora did now. *Will they make it? They seem so frail.*

But they had all made it, all except one or two, and Winslow had made it, and he, Louie, had made it.

EASY, BOY, EASY

Nora clapped her hands to her mouth each time she saw a new animal, as if she were trying to keep something inside from escaping. Louie watched her take it all in: the lambs; the tottering calf with its big head and curly fur; the pink squealing piglets. He had never seen Nora so animated.

Winslow pushed his muzzle through fence openings, introducing himself. The newborn calf and Winslow stood nose-to-nose, smelling each other, until the calf's mother mooed loudly and shoved Winslow's nose back through the fence, scolding him for getting too close to her baby.

The chickens fluttered and squawked and were not happy to see this new donkey creature near their shed, but they put on a showy display for Nora as she knelt near them. They strutted this way and that, clucking in quick bursts.

Louie had the odd feeling that something was missing, but he didn't know what that might be. He glanced around, trying to identify the missing piece.

They returned to the sheep pens and were watching the lambs still curled against their mother when the tractor returned to the barn and Uncle Pete called out to them.

Winslow's ears swiveled this way and that. He brayed loudly. From around the side of the house, a scruffy brown dog ambled lazily in their direction.

"Easy, boy, easy," Uncle Pete said to Winslow.

"Just my lazy old scaredy-cat watchdog, who is slow in realizing that visitors have approached. Check that tail wagging. Wouldn't frighten off a toad."

"We heard that donkeys and dogs don't get along," Louie said.

"Well, often that's the case, but this here old thing doesn't know he is a dog, and he doesn't seem to know that Winslow is a donkey either."

And then Louie knew what was missing. There had always been a donkey at the farm, a touchy, protective, and stubborn donkey. Uncle Pete had called it his LGD, and it was Gus who had said that LGD stood for Little Gray Donkey. That LGD was Winslow's mother.

SORRY!

The next day began well enough, with the sun shining in the windows, and Louie pulling on one of Gus's old jackets to wear to school, and his parents getting ready for work, and Winslow prancing around his pen and sniffing the air for spring scents. A day can begin so well.

But . . .

Mrs. Tooley came outside to scold Louie and his parents and Winslow, all of them, for "all that terrible noise, day and night!"

"But he doesn't usually bray at night," Louie tried. "Only occasionally."

"It's too much, I tell you, too much! I'm exhausted! I'm going crazy! Did that health person come? Did she tell you that animal can't stay here? Did the animal person come? Did he tell you the regulations?"

Louie's mother said, "They came. They told us."

His father said, "We're sorry you've been disturbed. We're taking care of it."

Louie did not say anything because his father had placed a cautioning hand on his shoulder, but what he was thinking was, *Your baby disturbs us! Your crying baby wakes me up!*

Shortly after Mrs. Tooley went back inside her house, Mack walked up the drive. He looked as if he were carrying a heavy weight on his back.

"What's the matter?" Louie asked.

"Claudine."

"Oh. Again?"

"She's breaking my heart, Louie."

Mack rubbed his hand down Winslow's neck and back. "I wish Gus were here," he said.

Louie and his parents silently nodded.

"I miss him," Mack said.

Louie and his parents continued to nod in silent agreement.

"I mean, I know protecting people and our country is important, and I know it's selfish to wish someone else had gone instead, but I *miss* him."

A sad and mournful and barely audible *eeee-awe* was Winslow's response.

Louie was unable to speak.

It rained the rest of the day.

SOMETHING WAS WRONG

That night, with the rain came the wind, powerful gusts howling through the trees. Twice Louie checked on Winslow to be sure he was secure and dry in his shelter. Thunder and lightning followed: sudden deep booms that shook the windows and sharp, bright, crackling light that lit up Louie's bedroom.

Louie crawled into Gus's bed and hid under the covers until the storm ceased and all was silent.

He hadn't slept long before he was awakened by the sound of Winslow braying.

Oh, no, Louie thought, *not now, not so loud, not in the middle of the night. Mrs. Tooley's baby will wake up and she will be mad.*

The braying continued, louder.

Oh, please, not now.

The braying was loud and relentless. Louie sat up. Something was wrong.

Louie's first thought as he reached the back door was that someone was taking Winslow and that Winslow was protesting.

Louie's father was already in the kitchen. "What a racket! What's going on?" he asked.

"Not sure, going to check." Louie grabbed a flashlight and headed outside.

The yard and pen were muddy from the rains. Straw was blown against the wire fencing and buckets were overturned. Winslow was kicking his back legs against the fence, agitated and insistent.

"Easy, boy, what's the matter?" Louie did not see or hear anyone. The gate was still latched. "What is it? Tell me."

As Louie opened the gate, Winslow lunged at him. He smelled of smoke. It seemed to be coming from the garage loft.

"Dad! Dad!"

The donkey pushed Louie away from the garage and into the yard, where he turned to the Tooleys' house and raised his head and brayed long and loud: *EEEE-AWE! EEEE-ONKA-AWE! EEEE-AWE!*

"It's okay, Winslow, okay, shh, quiet now—" but then he saw more smoke overhead. It was coming from the Tooleys' house.

PLEASE, PLEASE

As Winslow continued to bray, Louie banged on the Tooleys' back door. Overhead, the smoke increased, spewing from a hole in the Tooleys' roof and from their attic window.

And then Louie heard the baby wail and saw lights go on upstairs and then downstairs and at last Mrs. Tooley burst out the back door carrying the blanket-wrapped baby.

Winslow insisted on nudging the blanket,

murmuring in a small voice what sounded like *please, please.*

A flurry of sirens announced the arrival of fire trucks and within minutes the house was surrounded by firemen and ladders and hoses and water spraying through the air, lit up by streetlights in a yellow glow as the water arced toward the Tooleys' roof and Louie's garage.

Louie's parents and Mack and his family and dozens of other neighbors gathered nearby.

"The storm! The lightning!"

"Must've hit the roof!"

"Lucky you got out!"

"How did you—"

"When did you—"

Nora came running up the street, clad in rumpled pajamas and a sweatshirt. "I knew it!" she shouted. "I knew something was wrong!" She put her forehead right up against Louie's. "You okay?" When he nodded, she turned immediately to Winslow, wrapping her arms around his neck. She said the same to him, "You okay?"

Mrs. Tooley was still clutching her baby tightly and Winslow was still at her side, nudging her baby bundle.

"You!" Mrs. Tooley said to Winslow. "You noisy thing. You saved us."

BOOM-BOOM

After the firemen and Nora left, Mrs. Tooley and Louie's parents sat at the kitchen table in Louie's house. Mrs. Tooley was weepy and dazed. "Louie, do you mind checking on Boom-Boom?"

"Boom-Boom?"

"The baby. Boom-Boom."

"Um. That's his name?"

"Nickname."

Louie's mother said, "He's in your room. Mrs.

Tooley can sleep there, too. You can sleep downstairs tonight, okay?"

Louie tiptoed into his room, wary of waking
the baby, who was asleep in a portable crib that
had been placed between Louie's bed and Gus's.

Boom-Boom had chubby cheeks and long eyelashes, and on his head a tangled curly blob of
black hair that looked like a burnt cauliflower had
exploded there. One tiny hand clutched a corner of
the yellow blanket to his chin, and the thumb of
the other hand was snug in his mouth.

You are the cause of all that loud crying? Louie
thought.

Louie lightly placed his hand on the baby to
make sure he was breathing. He could feel the baby's
warmth and the gentle rise and fall of his chest.

Louie wondered if there was a Mr. Tooley
somewhere, and if there was, it must be hard to be
away from his son, and it must be hard for Mrs.
Tooley to be on her own.

And then he thought about Nora and wondered how hard it would be to have had a baby brother who didn't make it, and a dog who died too.

And he thought about Winslow, who never knew his mother, and how odd it would be to be raised by strangers who didn't speak your language.

Boom-Boom awoke, caught sight of Louie, and launched into a full-blown howl.

Immediately from outside came Winslow's loud bray.

Louie lifted the wailing Boom-Boom and carried him downstairs to Mrs. Tooley.

"Listen!" he said. "The baby cried *first*, and *then* Winslow started braying! Get it?"

Everyone looked puzzled.

"Winslow is a protector. He is braying *because* the baby is crying. Winslow is alerting people."

"Alerting people?" Mrs. Tooley asked.

"He's saying, 'The baby needs help! Protect the baby!'"

YOU'D BE PROUD

The kitchen was a busy place the next morning. Louie's parents were making coffee and pancakes, and Mrs. Tooley was feeding Boom-Boom, who was propped up in a baby chair, slapping his hands in cereal and rubbing it on his face and in his hair. Nora was taking it all in, having stopped by to check on Winslow.

In the middle of this, Uncle Pete clomped into the kitchen with a loud, "Hey, there!" He had heard about the fire, and he was making sure everyone was okay, but he also had other worries of his own. A coyote had taken one of the newborn lambs in the night.

"Terrible, terrible sight, what was left behind, I don't even want to tell you. Blood and mess and traumatized sheep."

Nora pressed a hand to her mouth and muttered, "Blech."

Louie felt as if something had dropped out of his chest, down through his legs and onto the floor. He didn't want to say anything, but the words came out of his mouth anyway.

"You need Winslow."

There was a moment of complete silence as everyone turned to Louie. Even Boom-Boom paused, with his hand in his mouth.

"Well, his mother *was* a good sheep protector," Uncle Pete admitted. "My LGD."

"Little Gray Donkey," Louie said.

"That's what Gus called her," Uncle Pete said, "but it usually stands for Livestock Guardian *Dog*. In my case, I had a Livestock Guardian *Donkey*."

Nora was staring hard at Louie. "You mean you could just let Winslow go?"

Louie turned to her. "Winslow would definitely make a loud ruckus if any critter tried to get near those sheep, right? He could be with other animals, and he'd have a purpose. He'd have an important job and he'd be good at it."

"You'd be proud of him," Uncle Pete said.

"And we could visit him, right?" Louie asked.

"Sure, whenever you want, every single day, if you like."

"Nora, too?"

"Sure."

THE BEST DONKEY

That day, Louie and Nora took Winslow for one last walk up to the top of the sledding hill, where they sat and ate bologna sandwiches while Winslow munched grass.

"He's a good donkey," Louie said.

"The best donkey," Nora added.

Winslow turned his head and gave them a long look before returning to his munching.

Louie said, "I talk to him all the time—not out

loud—but in my head, and he listens, and—don't laugh—but it seems as if he is talking to me, too."

"I do the same thing," Nora said. "He's very understanding."

Louie tossed part of his bread crust to Winslow, who gave it a sideways glance and returned to the grass in front of him, as if to say, "No thanks, I've got grass."

"I'll miss him," Louie said.

"But we can visit him, right? Your uncle Pete said so—we could go whenever we want."

"We could go every day if we wanted."

"After school, we could ride bikes out there. Except that—"

"What?"

"I don't have a bike."

"You can use mine. I'll use Gus's."

SETTLING IN

After school, Louie and Nora walked down the road with Winslow and through the town and all the way out to Uncle Pete's, where they reintroduced Winslow to the animals and to his new home with the sheep.

"Hey, there!" Uncle Pete said. "Want to help me with this?" He carried a tray with a syringe and vials. "Need to give that lamb its shots. Maybe you could hold it while I do that."

"Or *you* could hold it and *I* could give it the shots," Louie said. "I know how to do that now."

"Oh! Really? Well, sure then, go right ahead. I'll hold the lamb."

"Or *I* could hold the lamb, while Louie gives it the shots," Nora suggested.

Uncle Pete looked from one to the other, nodding. "That would be fine, just fine."

When Louie returned home, his parents were sitting on the front steps, holding the mail. Louie's mother waved a postcard.

"Guess who?"

The note was brief:

Hi, everybody—

News: Five days leave in July!

See you then!

Remember me?
Gus

Earlier that morning, Louie had thought he would feel infinitely sad on this day when he had to leave Winslow at the farm, but instead, as Winslow settled in with the ewe and her newborn lamb, and with news of Gus coming home, Louie felt that everything was as it should be.

THE LIGHT

As Louie fell asleep each night, he saw a slideshow in his mind: scenes moving by, some slowly, some quickly, some merging with others. The parade of images was different each night, offering up people and places in new combinations.

He often saw his parents and Gus and Mack and Claudine. He saw Uncle Pete and the farm and

Mrs. Tooley and her baby and a girl named Cookie. He saw an indigo bunting atop a golden sunflower, and he saw a thin man on a brown bench and a jacket-bear.

He saw Nora in her bumblebee coat and hat, and he heard her saying "I knew it!"

He saw a little gray donkey in his arms, and he saw Winslow with his mouth wide open, bellowing the strangest sounds, and he saw a lamb curled at Winslow's feet at the farm.

One night Louie was awakened by silvery light pouring in through his bedroom window. The light shone a path across the room and onto Gus's bed and the opposite wall with the painting of the boy and the calf.

He wondered if Gus was awake wherever he was and did he see this same light?

He wondered if Winslow was awake in his new home at the farm. Would the light be shining on the sign that Louie had added to Winslow's pen?

Remember me,
Louie

HEARTWARMING BOOKS BY
SHARON CREECH!